Sheltie
at the Funfair

Peter Clover

PUFFIN BOOKS

For Cissy and Missy

PUFFIN BOOKS

Published by the Penguin Group
Penguin Books Ltd, 80 Strand, London WC2R 0RL, England
Penguin Putnam Inc., 375 Hudson Street, New York, New York 10014, USA
Penguin Books Australia Ltd, 250 Camberwell Road, Camberwell, Victoria 3124, Australia
Penguin Books Canada Ltd, 10 Alcorn Avenue, Toronto, Ontario, Canada M4V 3B2
Penguin Books India (P) Ltd, 11 Community Centre, Panchsheel Park, New Delhi – 110 017, India
Penguin Books (NZ) Ltd, Cnr Rosedale and Airborne Roads, Albany, Auckland, New Zealand
Penguin Books (South Africa) (Pty) Ltd, 24 Sturdee Avenue, Rosebank 2196, South Africa

Penguin Books Ltd, Registered Offices: 80 Strand, London WC2R 0RL, England

www.penguin.com

First published 2001
7

Sheltie is a registered trademark owned by Working Partners Ltd
Copyright © Working Partners Ltd, 2001
All rights reserved

Created by Working Partners Ltd, London, W6 OQT

The moral right of the author has been asserted

Set in 14/22 Palatino

Made and printed in England by Clays Ltd, St Ives plc

Except in the United States of America, this book is sold subject to the condition that it shall not, by way
of trade or otherwise, be lent, re-sold, hired out, or otherwise circulated without the publisher's prior
consent in any form of binding or cover other than that in which it is published and without a similar
condition including this condition being imposed on the subsequent purchaser

British Library Cataloguing in Publication Data
A CIP catalogue record for this book is available from the British Library
ISBN 0-141-30805-2

Chapter One

'Sheep!' cried Emma as she dashed into the kitchen. 'There are *six* sheep in Sheltie's paddock. I've just seen them from my bedroom window!'

Mum was laying the table for breakfast. She looked across at Emma, who was struggling with her wellington boots, and gave a puzzled frown.

'Sheep?' she asked. 'In Sheltie's paddock?'

'Yes,' said Emma. 'And Sheltie's trying to round them up.'

Mum peered out the window. 'You're right,' she said. 'There are six ewes out there. Sheltie seems to be having a great time chasing them round in circles.'

Emma looked too. Her little Shetland pony had managed to bunch the sheep together into a tight group. Now he was herding the small flock towards the hedge at the side of the paddock.

Emma watched as Sheltie drove the sheep closer to the hedge. Then she gasped with surprise as the little pony chased them right into the foliage.

The sheep seemed to disappear, one by one, into the thick, green hedge.

'What?' cried Emma. She could hardly believe her eyes. She raced outside and

2

ran down to the paddock as fast as she
could.

Sheltie saw her coming and threw
back his head with a welcoming snort.

It was only when Emma had climbed
over the fence and into the paddock that
she saw where the sheep had gone.

There was a great big hole in Sheltie's

hedge. The sheep had scrambled through, back into Mr Brown's neighbouring field.

Emma ran up to Sheltie and held on to his shaggy mane. The last thing she wanted was for him to follow the flock into the open field.

'Come on, boy,' said Emma. She led Sheltie across to his field shelter, put on his head collar, and tethered him safely inside. Then she retraced her footsteps across the paddock and climbed through the hole in the hedge.

When Emma stepped into Mr Brown's field the six curious ewes scattered and fled to the far corners of their field. Emma made her way to the farmhouse and walked into the yard.

'Hello!' said Mr Brown. 'What can I

do for you today?' he asked when he
saw her frown.

'It's your sheep, Mr Brown,' said
Emma. 'They've chewed a great big hole
in Sheltie's hedge. And six of them have
already escaped into our paddock.'

'Oh dear,' said the farmer. 'Thank you

for telling me, Emma. I'd better come and fix it before any more escape. Or before Sheltie gets out!'

'I've never seen sheep in that field before,' remarked Emma.

'You're right.' Mr Brown smiled. 'I normally graze the sheep up in the top meadow, but there's a funfair coming to Little Applewood next week and I've rented out the lower field to them. I put the sheep there to crop the grass, ready for when the fair arrives next Saturday.'

'A funfair?' gasped Emma. 'Coming here to Little Applewood?' She couldn't wait to get back and tell Sheltie. It was the most exciting news she'd heard for ages.

Chapter Two

Mr Brown came over straight away to look at the big hole in Sheltie's hedge.

'It's huge,' said Mr Brown with a sigh. Sheltie seemed to think so too! He tossed back his head and blew a loud snort through his nostrils.

Emma held the little pony's reins loosely as the farmer examined the damage.

'You like the look of that hole, don't

you, Sheltie?' Emma grinned. 'It's just like a secret doorway leading to the other fields, isn't it?'

Mr Brown looked up. 'That's given me an idea,' he said. 'It's such a big hole, it could take months for the hedge to grow back. I could patch it up with some chicken wire … *or*, I could make the hole even bigger and put in a gate.'

'A gate!' exclaimed Emma. Sheltie's ears pricked up at the sound of her voice.

'A *private* gate,' said Mr Brown. 'So that you and Sheltie can let yourselves into my fields any time you like.'

'Our own private shortcut,' said Emma. 'It's a brilliant idea!'

Sheltie stomped his little legs in a patch of nettles. The little pony seemed to know that Emma was really excited about something.

'I've got an old wrought iron gate in one of the barns,' said Mr Brown. 'It has a strong lock with a key, and would look perfect here in the hedge.'

'Sheltie will be able to look out across the fields and the rolling hills,' added Emma. 'He'll like that!'

Sheltie flicked his mane in approval.

'He'll be able to see the funfair arrive as well,' said the farmer. 'And watch all the rides and sideshows being put up.'

Emma felt a shiver of excitement dancing along her spine as she thought about the funfair. She could hardly wait for the next few days to pass.

*

Saturday came around very quickly. Emma was so excited about the funfair that she woke up extra early. When she looked at her alarm clock it was only half past six. But Emma was wide awake and so was Sheltie. She could hear him outside in the paddock, blowing and snorting.

Emma leaped out of bed and rushed

to the bedroom window. Sheltie blew an even louder snort when he saw her standing there, as if to say, 'Where have *you* been – I've been calling you for ages.'

The sun had been up for a while too, and a low early-morning mist clung to the ground like a cloud.

Emma gave Sheltie a wave and blew him a kiss. Then she gasped as she saw why her little pony was making so much noise.

Beyond Sheltie's paddock, trundling slowly across Mr Brown's lower field, was an army of painted lorries and bright-coloured caravans. They moved quietly through the sunlit mist. The funfair had arrived!

Chapter Three

It was too early to wake anyone so Emma dressed quickly, and quietly let herself out of the cottage. She ran down the garden path and climbed over the wooden fence into Sheltie's paddock.

The little pony was already trotting across to his brand new field gate. He looked back over his withers to make sure that Emma was following.

Mr Brown had made an excellent job of the special gate. It fitted the hole in Sheltie's hedge perfectly and looked as if it had been there for years.

Sheltie gazed out over the rails with Emma. They watched the procession of vehicles park in an orderly line against the far hedgerow that bordered Bramble Thicket.

'Papa Girola's Travelling Funfair,' Emma read to Sheltie. The words were painted in swirling red and gold letters on the side of the big leading lorry, which was pulling a trailer.

'I wonder what's on that trailer,' said Emma. Sheltie rumbled a soft whicker and shook his mane. He seemed to be wondering too. But at the moment there was nothing to see. Whatever was on the trailer was covered with a heavy green tarpaulin.

'Look, Sheltie,' said Emma as she spotted the next lorry. 'There's a helter-skelter and a waltzer.' She looked from one lorry to the next, reading the names of the rides painted on the cab doors.

'Dodgem cars, flying saucers, a ghost train, a crooked house *and* a ferris wheel,' she said.

There were smaller lorries and vans too. Emma guessed that they carried the sideshows and stalls.

'I bet there's hoopla and a coconut shy and a candyfloss stall.' Sheltie's ears pricked up when Emma mentioned candyfloss.

'You like candyfloss, don't you, boy?' she said with a grin.

Sheltie gave a little whinny and licked his rubbery lips. Then he pushed his nose over the rails of the gate and took a big sniff of all the new smells in the air. His brown eyes twinkled brightly beneath his bushy forelock.

As Emma scanned the rows of parked

trailers and caravans, doors started to fly open and suddenly the field was busy with fairground folk.

Emma smiled as she noticed that her little pony was also watching everything with great interest. Then she realized what had caught Sheltie's eye. A young girl with lots of dark curly hair unhooked the tail flap of a trailer and led out a beautiful snow-white pony by its mane.

Sheltie pumped his little legs up and down with excitement and trampled a patch of daisies. The beautiful white pony lifted her head and caught Sheltie's scent on the morning breeze.

With a flick of her head, she pulled her mane free from the girl's grasp. But the pony didn't run off straight away. She looked at the girl first, and softly nudged her arm. Then she took off and galloped across the field towards Sheltie and Emma.

Chapter Four

Sheltie went right up to the field gate to greet the white pony.

Emma watched as Sheltie and his new friend rubbed noses and said hello in their special pony way.

'Oh, you're a real beauty, aren't you?' whispered Emma, and she reached over the gate to stroke the pony's silky neck.

Emma wasn't sure what she should

do. The girl in the field didn't seem at
all worried that her pony had run off. In
fact, she was smiling and walking
slowly towards them across the field.

Emma decided to keep the pony busy,
and scratched her soft ears until the girl
arrived. Sheltie was making funny
noises in his throat and trying to push
the gate open with his head.

'It's no good, Sheltie.' Emma smiled. 'I've got the key safely tucked away.' She touched the string around her neck. Two keys were hanging from it. One was for the field gate, and the other was for the padlock on the main gate into Sheltie's paddock. The little Shetland pony was very good at slipping bolts and escaping so Emma had to be extra careful that both gates were locked when she wasn't there.

'Hello,' said the girl brightly, pushing the dark curls off her face. She was a year or two older than Emma. 'I see you've already met Silva. My name's Bella. I'm with the fair.'

Emma smiled and introduced herself and Sheltie. 'We watched you all arrive, didn't we, boy?' Sheltie rubbed his muzzle against the gate rails and licked Bella's hand.

'He's a lovely Shetland pony, isn't he?' said Bella.

'The best!' Emma grinned. 'And Silva's a beauty too! Does she give rides at the fair?'

'Oh, no,' said Bella. 'She does much more than that. This is Silva the Amazing Vanishing Pony!'

'*Vanishing* pony,' gasped Emma. 'Did you hear that, boy?' Sheltie flicked his tail and whickered in Silva's ear.

'How does she vanish?' asked Emma.

Bella smiled cheekily and tossed her own dark mane of hair. 'You'll have to come along to the fair and see for yourself,' she said, throwing herself lightly up on to Silva's back. Then she

took a handful of silky mane and rode
bareback across the field to rejoin the
fairground folk.

'Don't forget to come and see us
tomorrow when we open,' called Bella
over her shoulder. 'I'll look out for you!'

'We'll be there,' Emma called back.
But Sheltie just blew a loud snort as he
watched the beautiful white mare gallop
away.

'Come on,' said Emma. 'You'll see Silva again soon. Let's get you some breakfast.'

Now *that* was a word that Sheltie liked. He flicked up his ears, then made a mad dash towards his field shelter and quickly disappeared inside.

Emma laughed to herself as she followed Sheltie – her own amazing vanishing pony!

Chapter Five

'It's a shame there's no carousel,' Emma
said to Sheltie. 'But everything else
looks great. I bet the fair will look
fantastic when it gets dark and all the
coloured lights come on.'

The fairground people had been
working really hard, and by midday
most of the rides and sideshows were
set up. Everything was arranged in a
neat circle, with a large empty space in

the middle. Everything, that is, except for the mysterious thing on the back of the big trailer. That was still hidden by the heavy green tarpaulin.

Sheltie began to paw at the grass. He pushed his muzzle over the gate rails, sniffing the air.

'I know which attraction *you* like the best,' said Emma, giggling. 'Silva the Amazing Vanishing Pony. I think you fancy Silva.' The little pony whickered softly as Emma ruffled his forelock. 'But I don't think you want to see Silva vanish, do you?'

Sheltie tossed his head back and sneezed.

'Well, *I* want to see how they make a pony vanish,' said Emma. 'And I bet Sally will too!' Sally was Emma's best friend, who lived nearby at Fox Hall Manor. 'We don't have long to wait,' continued Emma. 'The fair opens tomorrow!' She felt a flutter of excitement inside her tummy.

Emma was so busy daydreaming about which rides and sideshows she would visit first that she didn't notice that the big lorry and trailer had started to move.

It was Sheltie who saw it first. He nudged Emma's arm and blew a very loud snort.

'What is it, boy?' Emma followed Sheltie's gaze across the field and saw the lorry slowly backing out of its parking place.

'Oh, look,' she said excitedly. 'It's moving. I wonder what it is ...' Emma

watched the lorry make its way through
the circle of rides and sideshows to the
big empty space in the middle. 'It looks
like it's going to be the main attraction!'
she said.

Everyone at the funfair stopped what
they were doing to go and help. The
lorry came to a halt and two men
lowered the trailer tail flap to make a
long ramp.

Emma noticed that there were cables
attached to a large winch on the trailer.
These stopped the mystery ride from
whooshing down the ramp and crashing
to the ground. With an army of helpers
lending a hand to steady it, the ride slid
slowly down the ramp and took pride of
place in the centre of the funfair.

But Emma still couldn't see what it

was because the tarpaulin cover
remained fixed in place.

'Looks like we'll have to wait until
tomorrow to find out after all,' said

Emma, sounding a little disappointed.
But Sheltie blew a deafening snort in
her ear, as if to say, 'No, we don't.'

That gave Emma another thought.
'Why don't we just stroll over and say
hello, Sheltie? We could welcome the
fair to Little Applewood and ask about
the mystery ride.'

Suddenly, Sheltie gave a loud
whinny.

'I can guess who you've spotted,'
said Emma. She glanced into the field
and, sure enough, there was Bella on
her beautiful white pony, weaving in
and out of the caravans.

'She's riding bareback again,'
observed Emma. 'It looks like fun,
doesn't it, boy? Let's do the same and
go into the field.'

After fitting Sheltie's bridle, Emma unlocked the special gate. Then she led her little Shetland pony through the hedge and into the field, and rode bareback to join Bella and Silva.

Chapter Six

As soon as Bella saw Emma and Sheltie she came trotting over to say hello.

She sat tall on Silva's back and patted the pony's neck as she spoke to Emma. Sheltie was already busy blowing into Silva's nostrils.

'Have you come to take a peek at the rides?' asked Bella.

'We couldn't wait until tomorrow,' said Emma sheepishly, hoping that Bella and the other fairground people wouldn't mind. 'And we're dying to know what's under that big tarpaulin, aren't we, Sheltie?' The little pony pricked up his ears.

'It's Grandpapa Girola's Gallopers,' announced Bella with a smile. 'Grandpapa owns the funfair and the Gallopers are his pride and joy.'

'What are the Gallopers?' asked Emma. 'Is it a ride?'

'I'll show you,' said Bella. 'I'll fetch Grandpapa and we'll show you together. It's time the tarpaulin came off.'

Papa Girola was a kind-looking man with a smiling face and a mop of silver-grey hair. Everyone except Bella called him Papa Girola. He ruffled Sheltie's mane and winked at Bella.

'So you want to see the Gallopers?' he said cheerfully to Emma and Sheltie. 'We always save the best until last, when all the other rides are set up. It's very special to us, you see.'

'The Gallopers used to belong to Grandpapa's father,' explained Bella. 'And every year they help us to win the Carnival Chalice.'

Emma's eyes grew to the size of saucers as she tried to imagine just *what* the Gallopers might be.

Sheltie had stopped nuzzling up to Silva now and was suddenly interested in Bella's grandfather. He was wearing a colourful patchwork waistcoat, which smelled of candyfloss.

The little pony nibbled at one of the pockets and made it all wet. But Papa

Girola didn't seem to mind.

'It's my lucky waistcoat,' he said. 'I always wear it when we set up the rides – to bring luck to the fair. But it's let me down recently,' he sighed.

'We've had some rotten luck,' explained

Bella. 'At the last two sites there were a few mishaps –'

'But your friend doesn't want to hear about *that*,' interrupted Papa Girola. 'She's come to see the Gallopers. So let's show them to her.'

Bella slipped lightly from Silva's back and helped her grandfather with the tarpaulin. The cover was held in place with three guide ropes.

Papa Girola offered a rope to Emma. 'Do you feel like giving us a hand?' he asked.

'You bet,' said Emma. She took the rope and looped it around her hand. Bella and Papa Girola held the other two ropes.

'On the count of three,' announced Bella.

Then she counted and they pulled.

Sheltie blew a surprised whinny and Emma gasped with delight as the heavy tarpaulin slid away.

Underneath was the most beautiful merry-go-round that Emma had ever seen.

Chapter Seven

'A carousel,' breathed Emma.

Beautiful carved wooden horses stood prancing beneath a multi-coloured canopy. Striped red poles rose from the Gallopers' saddles and disappeared into a ceiling of glowing lights.

'It's fantastic,' said Emma. But when Emma looked at Bella and her grandfather, she could tell that something was wrong. Sheltie seemed to sense something too and blew a low whicker.

'The heads!' exclaimed Bella. 'Two of the Gallopers' heads have been knocked off.'

It was true. Two of the horses' wooden heads were lying smashed on the wooden boards of the carousel floor.

'Who would do such a horrible thing?' asked Emma.

'The same person who's been following the fair for the past two months,' muttered Papa Girola. 'Someone seems determined to ruin our chances of winning the Carnival Chalice.'

'And you've no idea who it could be?' said Emma.

'No idea at all,' Papa Girola said anxiously.

'Things keep getting smashed and broken,' added Bella. 'This is the second time they've picked on the carousel – and we need it to win the Chalice.'

'What do you have to do to win?' asked Emma.

'We're judged on the quality and content of the fair, and given points for the most exciting and original rides,' replied Papa Girola.

'A team of judges travels the country, visiting all the small fair sites in the competition,' explained Bella.

'And it's the carousel that normally wins the Chalice for us,' added a dark-haired man who was standing nearby.

'This is my Uncle Beppe,' said Bella.

'He helps my father make Silva disappear in the sideshow, don't you, Uncle?'

Beppe smiled and ruffled Bella's hair. 'I wish I could make whoever's doing this damage to our fair disappear,' he growled. 'The judges are coming here in three days' time and now we've got even more work to do.'

'Then we'd better get started with the repairs,' said Papa Girola to his youngest son. 'It was nice to meet you, Emma. I hope you'll be coming to the fair when we open tomorrow?'

'Oh, I will,' said Emma eagerly. 'I wouldn't miss it for the world.'

Sheltie pricked up his ears excitedly. He seemed to think that he was going to the fair too!

The next afternoon Mr Jones drove his
daughter, Sally, over to Emma's house.

All of Emma's family were going to
the funfair, and Sally was going with
them.

Emma's little brother, Joshua, was
really excited. He'd never been to a fair
before.

Sheltie had been watching the funfair
all day. He had been standing at his
field gate, listening to the lively
fairground music, with his ears perky
and alert.

When Emma, Sally, Mum, Dad and
Joshua came walking across his
paddock Sheltie went trotting over to
meet them.

Emma gave him a big hug and a fuss,

41

then unlocked the gate in the hedge as he stood by, pumping his little legs up and down excitedly.

'Sorry, boy,' said Emma as she held the gate open for everyone else to pass through. 'You've got to stay here. I'm afraid ponies aren't allowed at the fair.'

Sheltie gave a soft snort as though he

understood that he couldn't go to the fair with Emma and the rest of the family.

'Poor Sheltie,' said Joshua.

'But we won't be long,' soothed Mum.

As Emma pulled the iron gate closed behind her Sheltie pushed his nose between the rails and blew a pitiful whicker.

'Oh, don't be sad, Sheltie,' pleaded Emma. 'I'll be back by teatime. I know you want to come too, but a funfair isn't the best place for a pony.'

Sheltie answered by blowing a raspberry. Then Dad called, 'Come on, Emma. Don't get left behind.' And Emma hurried off.

As they crossed the field the fairground music grew louder and louder. Emma could see the big ferris wheel turning above the tented canopies of the other rides. She could hear the happy screams and laughter of all the fairground visitors.

They walked slowly into the heart of the funfair, and Emma and Sally looked around with their mouths and eyes open wide. There was so much to see. The waltzer cars waltzed. The dodgem cars dodged. The flying saucers flew and the ghost train howled. Everywhere they looked, something was happening.

Then Emma heard the magical organ music of the carousel. She looked around and saw that the Gallopers were turning slowly, bobbing up and down on their striped poles. Each wooden Galloper carried a rider on its back.

'They've fixed it!' exclaimed Emma excitedly. 'They've fixed the Gallopers. Every rider has got a perfect mount.'

'It looks fantastic!' said Sally. 'Shall we have a go?'

Emma was about to say yes, when she spotted a very special sideshow. It was called *Silva the Amazing Vanishing Pony*. The words were painted in swirly silver letters on a board above the entrance to a big tent.

'*See a live pony vanish before your very eyes,*' boasted another sign.

'It's Bella's sideshow,' said Emma. 'Oh, Sally, we've just got to see *that* first.'

Sally agreed straight away. Emma had told her all about Bella and Silva.

'We're going to try and win a fluffy

45

tiger for Joshua at the hoopla stall,' said
Mum. 'We'll see you over there by the
helter-skelter in half an hour.'

'OK,' said Emma. Then she grabbed
Sally's arm and dragged her towards
the tent.

Bella was at the entrance selling
tickets with her father. Inside there was
quite a crowd. Everyone was seated on
rows of wooden benches. Emma and
Sally sat at the front. They had an
excellent view of the small stage, which
was draped mysteriously with black
curtains.

A shiver of excitement ran down
Emma's back as Angelo, Bella's father,
walked out on to the stage.

'Ladies and gentlemen,' he began.
'You are about to witness an extraordinary

feat of magic never to be seen outside these tented walls.'

The audience were silent with anticipation.

'May I present to you … Silva the Amazing Vanishing Pony.'

There was a round of applause, then Uncle Beppe led Silva on to the stage. The curtains suddenly flew back to reveal a big gilded cage with an open door. Silva was led inside.

She stood, ghostly and pale, behind the metal bars – a mystical, magical mare.

Angelo pulled a different curtain around the cage, and a bright light came on, outlining Silva as a black silhouette against the material. Then there was a blinding flash and the silhouette vanished. The curtain flew back and all that was left was an empty gilded cage.

The audience gasped. Then they clapped and cheered noisily.

Bella's father drew the curtain around the cage again, and the light came back on, as before. Now all Emma and Sally could see was the silhouette of the empty cage.

Again, a brilliant flash. But this time nothing happened – Silva didn't re-appear. Instead, Bella came running out on to the stage yelling, 'She's gone! Silva's really gone. She's vanished.'

Emma looked around as the audience laughed like crazy. They all seemed to think it was part of the act. Emma wasn't so sure.

Then a truly amazing thing happened. The silhouette of a pony suddenly appeared in the cage … but it wasn't Silva. It was definitely the silhouette of a Shetland pony. Angelo

pulled back the curtains, and there
stood Sheltie.

Chapter Eight

Emma and Sally gasped in disbelief as the applause from the audience roared in their ears.

'Sheltie!' breathed Emma. 'But how did he get there?' she wondered out loud. 'And where is Silva?'

Bella ran outside in a panic with her father as the audience pushed and shoved their way through the exit. Emma and Sally quickly made their way to the stage to let Sheltie out of the cage.

The little pony seemed really pleased to have found Emma. But Emma couldn't understand how Sheltie had escaped from his paddock in the first place. 'I was in such a hurry,' she told Sally. 'Maybe I didn't lock the gate properly.' The Shetland pony blew a really loud raspberry, then started sniffing and licking the bars of the cage.

Bella came rushing back in with her father. 'Silva's gone!' she cried. 'We can't find her anywhere.'

'But she couldn't have really vanished,' exclaimed Emma.

Angelo put his arm around Bella and explained the trick to Emma and Sally. 'There's a false back to the cage, which drops away when the lights flash on,' he said. 'Then fake bars drop down to make the cage look solid again. It all happens very quickly,' he added. 'Beppe holds Silva backstage and waits. When the lights flash for the second time he sends her back up the ramp and into the cage, through the fake bars.'

'Only someone was hiding backstage,' sobbed Bella. 'They knocked Uncle Beppe on the head, and now they've stolen Silva.'

Uncle Beppe came in, rubbing his sore head.

'I didn't see anyone,' he muttered. 'It's very dark backstage. One moment I was holding Silva ... then the next moment I was lying on the floor seeing stars. And Silva was gone.'

'You *must* have forgotten to lock the

gate, Emma,' said Sally. 'Then Sheltie must have escaped from his paddock and wandered backstage, looking for you.'

Emma ruffled Sheltie's shaggy mane. 'And then he must have walked up the ramp and through the fake bars into the cage at just the right moment. Is that what you did, boy?'

The little pony nudged Emma's tummy and blew a soft snort into her sweatshirt.

'But what about Silva?' cried Bella. 'Where *is* she? We've got to find her.'

'Perhaps you should call the police,' suggested Sally.

'No!' snapped Uncle Beppe sharply. 'We like to take care of things like this ourselves, here at the fair.'

'Perhaps we can help,' offered Emma.
'I can saddle Sheltie up and go looking
for Silva.'

'She can't be very far away,' said
Sally. 'Unless she's been taken away in a
horsebox.'

'I'll take Sheltie home and tack him
up,' said Emma. 'Will you tell Mum and
Dad where I've gone, Sally?' Then she
was off, riding Sheltie bareback across
the field to the paddock.

Emma found the field gate wide open.

'So you found out that I forgot to lock
the gate, did you?' She grinned.

Sheltie answered by blowing a cheeky
raspberry, then sniffed at the air as
Emma closed and locked the gate
behind them. She was about to leave
Sheltie in the paddock while she went to

fetch his saddle and bridle from the tack
room. But the little pony started to act
strangely. His ears pricked up suddenly
and he tossed his shaggy head, sniffing
the air with deep snorts.

'What is it, Sheltie?' asked Emma, stopping in her tracks. 'What's wrong?' But before she even had time to look round, the little pony raced across the paddock and disappeared into his field shelter.

Emma flew after him. 'Sheltie, what is it? What are you up to?' she called as she followed him inside. Then she gasped at what she saw.

Chapter Nine

Sheltie was standing in the far corner of the shelter, nuzzling a beautiful white pony. Silva had found her way to Sheltie's paddock and was hiding in his shelter.

'Silva! What are you doing here?' said Emma. Then she saw a dirty mark across the pony's white rump. It looked as if someone had smacked her with a stick.

Sheltie blew a sympathetic whicker and licked Silva's muzzle.

'You poor thing,' sighed Emma. 'Whoever knocked Bella's Uncle Beppe on the head must have done this to frighten you away. But at least you're safe now. What a clever pony to find your way here to Sheltie's field shelter.'

Emma turned to Sheltie. 'You'll look after Silva while I go and fetch Bella and Mr Girola, won't you, boy?'

The little pony shook out his long mane and stood on guard across the entrance of the shelter while Emma ran all the way back to the fairground.

After Emma told Bella and her father the news, they rushed back to Sheltie's paddock to make sure that Silva was OK. They agreed that it would be best if Silva stayed with Sheltie for a while.

'Whoever is trying to ruin Grandpapa's funfair might come back after Silva again,' said Bella anxiously, when they were all back at the fair.

'She'll be safe with Sheltie in the paddock,' assured Emma. 'No one will think of looking for Silva there, away from the fair.'

'We'll be moving on in a few days' time,' said Angelo. 'Once the judges have been and looked around the fairground, we'll be off and away. And Silva can come with us then.'

'But what if this mysterious troublemaker follows you again?' asked Mum.

'I'm an old man,' replied Papa Girola. 'I've been with the fair all my life and you get used to trouble of one kind or another. But this is one problem I shall be happy to say goodbye to when we leave Little Applewood.'

Emma and Sally looked puzzled. Bella explained. 'Grandpapa is following an old family tradition and passing the fair on to his oldest child when we leave here,' she said. 'And *that's* my father! He's going to be the new fairground owner. And one day he'll pass it on to me.'

'Wow!' gasped Emma. 'You mean one day you'll own this whole funfair?'

Bella beamed a huge smile and gave her father a hug. 'But it won't be for years and years,' she added shyly.

'And until then you've got to help your father as much as you can,' said Papa Girola. He ruffled his granddaughter's hair, then turned to Emma and Sally. 'Now, what are you two standing here for? There's a whole fairground full of rides just waiting for you,' he said.

'Come on then, Sally,' said Emma,

grinning. 'The Gallopers or the ghost train?'

'The Gallopers! Let's go!' said Sally.

'Wait for me!' cried Bella.

'This is brilliant,' Emma whooped as the brightly painted Galloper she was riding rose and rolled in time to the piped organ music.

'It's fantastic,' agreed Sally. Her horse galloped along between Emma's and Bella's. As the carousel went round and round the three girls waved to everyone.

Little Joshua was jumping up and down, clapping his hands. He was going to have a ride next, with Dad. He waved as Emma's horse passed by.

Mum waved too, and so did Papa Girola and Angelo. But when Emma waved to Uncle Beppe, he didn't even smile. He just looked down at his boots. Then he turned his back to them and walked away into the crowd.

Chapter Ten

The next day Emma took Sheltie
out for a quick ride with Bella and
Silva.

'Don't be too long,' said Mum as
Emma pulled on her riding hat. 'Your
tea will be ready in half an hour.'

'OK,' called Emma as she raced out of
the back door.

Sheltie and Silva had become very
good friends. The little Shetland pony

was really enjoying having Silva for company in his paddock. Now he was pumping his little legs up and down excitedly, waiting to be tacked up for a ride.

Bella always rode her pony bareback, but she did use a bridle, reins and a hat when she was riding outside the fairground.

The two girls chatted as they trotted along side by side, down the country lane.

'What time are the judges coming tomorrow?' asked Emma. She felt sad knowing that the funfair would soon be leaving Little Applewood.

Bella clapped Silva's arched neck. 'We're the last fair to be judged in the competition,' she replied. 'The judges have been travelling around the country for weeks. Grandpapa says that they should be coming at about six o'clock. He wants to make sure that everything is running like clockwork when he opens the fair for the last time.'

Emma remembered that Papa Girola was handing the funfair over to Bella's father as soon as the judges had left.

'I hope you win the Carnival Chalice,' said Emma. 'I think your funfair is brilliant – and the Gallopers must be the best carousel in the whole world!'

'Grandpapa's really worried about the Gallopers,' confessed Bella. 'It's been vandalized twice this month, and each time the damage gets worse. He's putting it back under cover again until tomorrow afternoon.'

'I wonder who's doing it,' puzzled Emma. 'I bet Sheltie knows.' The little pony flicked up his ears when he heard his name, and Emma ruffled his mane. 'Sheltie probably saw the culprit the other day when he knocked your Uncle Beppe on the head and drove Silva away,' said Emma. 'It's a pity he can't tell us who the culprit is.'

The following day Sheltie was on his best behaviour. He had been playing with Silva all day in the paddock. Now he seemed ready for a nice, quiet ride.

'Come on, boy,' called Emma. 'Let's go and visit Bella. It's our last chance to see the fair before it leaves tomorrow. I know that funfairs aren't the best places for ponies, but you will be good, won't you, boy?'

Sheltie jangled his bit and stood patiently while Emma opened the field gate for him.

'I wonder if the carnival judges have been yet?' Emma said to Sheltie. Then she remembered that they weren't due until six o'clock. She urged Sheltie on, and he trotted towards the fairground.

As Emma rode Sheltie between two sideshows she saw Bella's Uncle Beppe ducking behind the candyfloss stand. He had something in his hand. Emma couldn't see what it was, but she did see him push it under the base of the stall. Then she watched him hurry away.

What *was* he doing? wondered Emma. But before she had a chance to think

about it, she saw that the tarpaulin was
about to be pulled off the carousel.

'Come on, Sheltie,' she whispered.
'Let's go and watch too!'

But as the tarpaulin was dragged

clear, Emma gasped in horror. An eerie silence swept across the crowd as everyone stared at the Gallopers.

Chapter Eleven

'Oh, no!' whispered Emma. The Gallopers had been vandalized again. But this time the damage was far, far worse than before.

Several poles were broken. Two horses had had their tails cut away, and another had had a front leg snapped off. But, worst of all, one Galloper was completely smashed to pieces.

'Who could do such a thing?' asked one of the fairground visitors.

'Someone with a hammer. And with a nasty grudge!' said Angelo angrily.

Poor Papa Girola looked very upset. 'The carnival judges will be here any minute,' he sighed. 'We don't stand a chance of winning now.'

'Oh yes we do,' said Bella fiercely. 'Whoever did this isn't going to stop us. We're still the best small fair in the country, and we're going to win that Chalice. If we don't try then whoever did this has beaten us,' she added.

'Bella's right,' announced Papa Girola. 'Come on, everyone. Let's put this mess in order.'

Emma leaped out of Sheltie's saddle to go and help. While she was picking up bits of horsehair and splintered wood she saw Sheltie slowly wander off.

Emma noticed that he was nosing around the base of the candyfloss stall. Soon he came trotting back to her with something clamped between his teeth.

'What's that you've got, boy?' asked Emma.

Sheltie snorted and dropped a hammer on to the grass in front of her. The tool's blunt head was marked heavily with red paint. It was the same colour red as the poles on the carousel and the pattern on the smashed Galloper.

Bella rushed over to Emma's side. 'That's Uncle Beppe's hammer!' she exclaimed. 'I'd know it anywhere. It's got a "B" carved into the handle.'

Everyone stopped what they were doing and looked around for Bella's

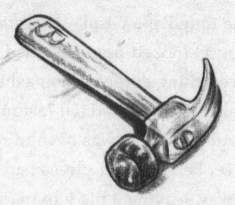

uncle. But he had disappeared into his caravan.

Emma told Papa Girola how she and Sheltie had seen Uncle Beppe hide something under the stall. 'It must have been the hammer,' she said.

'I'm going to have a word with that son of mine,' growled Papa Girola. And he marched off towards the parked caravans.

Emma watched as the fairground folk worked hard to fix the damage.

By the time Papa Girola had returned, the carousel looked *nearly* as good as new. Everything except the smashed Galloper had been fixed. Unfortunately, that particular horse was beyond repair. All the broken bits and pieces had been taken away, leaving a big gap in the middle of the carousel.

When Papa Girola saw the star ride he covered his eyes with his hand.

'We won't win anything now,' he groaned in despair. 'The Gallopers are famous. The carousel will be the first thing the carnival judges look at when they get here.'

Sheltie suddenly blew a really loud snort and shook his reins to attract Emma's attention.

'What is it, boy?' asked Emma. She

followed Sheltie's gaze to a small group of people walking towards them from across the field.

'It's the judges!' cried Papa Girola. 'Quick, everyone. Start the carousel. Play the music and get some riders on the Gallopers. With a bit of luck, they just might not notice.'

Suddenly the carousel sprang into life as the judges stepped through the ring of sideshows in front of the dancing Gallopers.

Emma looked around for Sheltie. But her little pony was nowhere to be seen.

Chapter Twelve

'Where could Sheltie have gone?' said
Emma.

'He was here a second ago,' answered
Bella.

Emma's eyes searched the crowds.
Then something made her look back at
the carousel as it played and turned
before the examining judges.

'Sheltie!' Emma gasped in disbelief.
The little Shetland pony had climbed up

on to the carousel and was standing
perfectly still in the empty space
between two of the Gallopers.

'What a marvellous idea!' exclaimed
the head judge. 'How clever to put that
model of a little Shetland pony amongst
the wooden horses.'

'It looks so real,' said another judge.

Sheltie didn't blink an eyelid or
move a muscle as the carousel sent him
sailing past. He stood very still and
went round again … and again … and
again.

'It's the most original idea I've seen
for a long time,' said the third judge.
They all made notes on their clipboards,
then moved away to inspect the rest of
the funfair.

The carousel stopped turning and

Sheltie clambered off with a satisfied snort.

'Oh, Sheltie!' cried Emma. 'You were brilliant.'

'The judges thought Sheltie was part of the carousel,' said Bella, laughing delightedly.

'And he was! He was the best Galloper on the carousel,' said a voice from behind them.

Emma and Sheltie looked around. It was Uncle Beppe looking very sorry for himself after his chat with Papa Girola.

'I'm afraid I've been very stupid,' he said, looking over at his older brother, Angelo. 'I was jealous at the idea of the funfair being passed on to you,' he explained. 'I've worked all my life with you on the fair, and an old family

tradition means that I will never be able
to share or own any part of it.'

Emma looked at Bella, and Sheltie
cocked his head to one side as though
he was listening too.

'It was me who kept breaking things

and vandalizing the Gallopers,' Uncle Beppe confessed. 'I thought that if it looked as though someone was following the fair and smashing the rides then you wouldn't want to own it – or at least not by yourself. I hoped that maybe you would ask me to share the worry and the problems. I thought you might share the responsibility of the funfair ... and make me a partner. But I didn't account for Sheltie.'

The little pony pawed at the ground and blew a raspberry at Uncle Beppe.

'It was Sheltie who found the hammer,' said Emma. 'And he must have recognized you the other afternoon when he swapped places with Silva at the sideshow.'

'He *did*,' admitted Uncle Beppe. 'I

wanted the act to go wrong, so I drove Silva away. I even hit myself on the head with a piece of wood to make it look as if I'd been attacked. But then Sheltie turned up and took Silva's place. My plan was spoiled because the audience loved it. They all thought it was part of the act – thanks to Sheltie.'

The little pony looked very pleased with himself.

'And you went to all this trouble because you were jealous?' asked Angelo.

Uncle Beppe nodded. He looked so sad. Suddenly, Bella ran up to him and threw her arms around his waist. She looked back at her father pleadingly. 'Can Uncle Beppe be a partner in the funfair. Please?' she asked. 'Can't we change the family tradition?'

Bella's father smiled. 'Of course he can. There's more than enough work and worry for two people. I only wish he had come to me first and asked, instead of messing with the rides.'

Just then the judges came strolling back.

'Quick, Emma,' said Bella. 'Can you get Sheltie back up on the carousel?'

Emma led her little pony up on to the big merry-go-round and sat in his saddle.

'Stand still, boy … *Please!*' whispered Emma.

Sheltie was fantastic. He didn't move a hair or twitch a nostril as the judges announced their verdict.

'We've seen all the travelling fairs now,' said the chief judge, 'and we've decided that Papa Girola's Travelling Funfair has won the Carnival Chalice yet again.'

A huge cheer went up from the gathering crowd as the carousel started turning again.

'As usual the presentation will take place at the Showman's Ball next month,' said the second judge.

'We look forward to seeing you there,' said the third. Then they breezed out of the fairground, back to their waiting car.

'Now I can retire a happy man,' said Papa Girola with a grin. 'Thanks to that clever little pony of yours, Emma.'

The carousel went round and round,

with Sheltie in pride of place among the Gallopers. His bright eyes twinkled beneath his bushy mane and he blew a raspberry each time he passed Uncle Beppe.

'I suppose I deserve that from Sheltie, don't I?' he said sheepishly to Angelo. 'But I promise everyone that I'll do my very best from now on to make sure that The Girola Brothers' Travelling Funfair remains the *best* in the country. And we'll win that Chalice again next year – you'll see.'

Emma felt so proud of Sheltie. He'd helped to solve a big family problem, and he'd won the Carnival Chalice for the Girola family.

The carousel turned again and the smallest Galloper threw up his head as he passed. Only this time, he gave an extra loud whinny that could be heard from every corner of the fairground.

If you like making friends, fun, excitement
and adventure, then you'll love

The little pony with the big heart!

Sheltie is the lovable little Shetland pony with a big
personality. He is cheeky, full of fun and has a heart
of gold. His owner, Emma, knew that she and Sheltie
would be best friends as soon as she saw him. She
could tell that he thought so too by the way his
brown eyes twinkled beneath his big, bushy mane.
When Emma, her mum and dad and little brother,
Joshua, first moved to Little Applewood, she thought
that she might not like living there. But life is
never dull with Sheltie around. He is full of
mischief and he and Emma have lots of exciting
adventures together.

Share Sheltie and Emma's adventures in:

SHELTIE THE SHETLAND PONY
SHELTIE SAVES THE DAY
SHELTIE AND THE RUNAWAY
SHELTIE FINDS A FRIEND
SHELTIE TO THE RESCUE
SHELTIE IN DANGER

to the Rescue

The little pony with the big heart!

Emma thinks that going to Summerland Bay
will be the best holiday ever – especially as
Sheltie can come too. Emma can't believe it
when she sees snobby Alice Parker. She is
always making fun of Sheltie. But when Alice
and her pony get into trouble, Sheltie is the
only one who can save them.

READ MORE IN PUFFIN

For children of all ages, Puffin represents quality and variety – the very best in publishing today around the world.

For complete information about books available from Puffin – and Penguin – and how to order them, contact us at the appropriate address below. Please note that for copyright reasons the selection of books varies from country to country.

On the World Wide Web: www.penguin.co.uk

In the United Kingdom: Please write to *Dept. EP, Penguin Books Ltd, Bath Road, Harmondsworth, West Drayton, Middlesex UB7 ODA*

In the United States: Please write to *Penguin Putnam inc., P.O. Box 12289, Dept B, Newark, New Jersey 07101-5289* or call 1-800-788-6262

In Canada: Please write to *Penguin Books Canada Ltd, 10 Alcorn Avenue, Suite 300, Toronto, Ontario M4V 3B2*

In Australia: Please write to *Penguin Books Australia Ltd, P.O. Box 257, Ringwood, Victoria 3134*

In New Zealand: Please write to *Penguin Books (NZ) Ltd, Private Bag 102902, North Shore Mail Centre, Auckland 10*

In India: Please write to *Penguin Books India Pvt Ltd, 11 Panscheel Shopping Centre, Panscheel Park, New Delhi 110 017*

In the Netherlands: Please write to *Penguin Books Netherlands bv, Postbus 3507, NL-1001 AH Amsterdam*

In Germany: Please write to *Penguin Books Deutschland GmbH, Metzlerstrasse 26, 60594 Frankfurt am Main*

In Spain: Please write to *Penguin Books S. A., Bravo Murillo 19, 1° B, 28015 Madrid*

In Italy: Please write to *Penguin Italia s.r.l., Via Felice Casati 20, I-20124 Milano*

In France: Please write to *Penguin France S. A., 17 rue Lejeune, F-31000 Toulouse*